Walt Disney's
AMERICAN CLASSICS
Paul Bunyan

Twin Books

MALLARD PRESS

Early one morning after a ferocious storm, a huge cradle washed up near a town in Maine. Inside the cradle was the biggest baby anyone had ever seen. It took the milk of five cows to fill his bottle!

The townfolk adopted him and named him Paul Bunyan, because they thought he should have the kind of name that sounded like a big guy's name!

Paul grew into a good lad and everybody liked him. He went to school just like all the other kids, but he was too big to fit inside the classrooom. So he sat outside and handed his lessons to the teacher by lifting the roof.

When school let out, all the kids would head for the old swimming hole. For huge Paul it was more like a bathtub!

Paul was interested in a lot of things as a youngster, but as he got older and bigger, he spent more and more time in the woods watching the loggers cut trees.

The townfolk noticed Paul's fascination with logging, and on his
...enth Christmas they gave him a present that was to change his
...rever and turn him into a legend.
...as a great, big, beautiful axe—just the right size!

big double-bladed axe, Paul could cut trees faster than
ut weeds.
Paul logged he was followed by prospective farmers, for
ear enough land for a whole farm *in one day*.

ged so fast that soon most of the forests were cut, and
ed in and built towns using lumber made from the logs
nd his fellow loggers had cut.
e East was getting too citified for a fellow like Paul, who
ree axe handles tall, so one day he headed west, in
ore forests and new adventures.

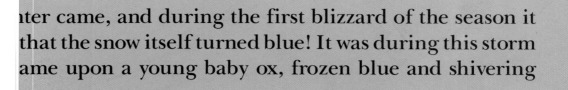

nter came, and during the first blizzard of the season it
that the snow itself turned blue! It was during this storm
ame upon a young baby ox, frozen blue and shivering

ig guy," said Paul, picking him up under one arm and
n close to try to thaw him out.

er he'd thawed out,
stayed blue.
such a cute fella," said Paul, "I
all you Babe—Babe the Blue Ox!"
ew fast, and overnight he was twice
barn. Paul thought it was great to
as big as he was. So did Babe!

Not only was Babe Paul's closest companion, but he was mighty strong, too.

When Paul set up his logging camp near a river that had too many bends in it to float logs, he tied a length of rope and an anchor to Babe's yoke, and Babe pulled that river straight as a pine log!

Paul and Babe kept moving westward. As they were passing through Minnesota, they got confused during a ferocious rainstorm. Completely lost, they wandered around in circles for days.

The big puddles left by their footprints remained full of water, and to this day people still call Minnesota "The Land of Ten Thousand Lakes."

nd of the summer, Paul and Babe had reached Wyoming.
 so glad to finally be out West that they got into a friendly
 match, and they kicked up a whole mountain range,
ow called the Grand Tetons. After the match they were
ty, so Paul found a big mountain stream which he used to
ower bath for him and Babe. When they'd finished, they
nd left it running, and it's now called Yellowstone Falls.

Out West among the giant trees there were big logging camps that were just the kind of places for Paul.

Now the loggers were big eaters. The head cook, Sourdough Sam, and his crew of forty served up hotcakes stacked to the ceiling, mountains of ten pound steaks and biscuits by the cart-load.

But no one was a bigger eater than Paul Bunyan, so Sourdough Sam's men made special six-foot doughnuts for him—and, of course, for Babe, too.

Babe got special treatment from Ole Olson, the camp black-smith. The ox shoes he made for Babe were so heavy that when Ole lifted them, his feet sank deep in the ground.

ot summer day, Paul brought a load of corn into camp, and
grew so hot in the scorching sun it began to pop.
blizzard!" cried the men, and they bundled up and shivered
ght of it. A herd of cattle took one look at the blizzard and
lue on the spot!

that fall the skeeter bees were flying North and South—they
n't remember which direction to go, since they had a bee
r on one end and a "skeeter" stinger on the other.
ir buzzing became louder and louder as a stranger came
ing into camp aboard a shiny new locomotive.

name," said the stranger, "is Joe Muffaw, and I'm
show you something you won't believe. I've got an
atic tree-cutting machine and a log-pulling
otive that'll do your work in half the time."
was angry. "Out *here* we use a double-bladed axe
ting and oxen for pulling, Little Fella."

But Joe Muffaw continued to brag, so a contest was organized to see who could pull a triple load of logs faster—the locomotive, or Babe the Blue Ox.

"Come on, Babe!" cried the loggers, as he and the locomotive pulled with all their might, snorting and puffing.

When it was over...

... Babe lost by half an inch.

Sadly, Paul and Babe decided to say "So long" to their friends and head North.

hatever happened to Paul Bunyan and Babe? Well, some folks
hat logging machines put Paul out of business. Others say that
felt crowded, and went to Alaska, where the logging is endless
a man and his ox have plenty of room.

you're sixty-three axe handles high like Paul, you need a lot
om!

First published in the United States of
America in 1989 by The Mallard Press.

Mallard press and its accompanying design
and logo are trademarks of
BDD Promotional Book Company, Inc.
Produced by
Twin Books
15 Sherwood Place
Greenwich, CT 06830

ISBN 0-792-45056-6

Designed, edited and illustrated by
American Graphic Systems, San Francisco

Printed in Hong Kong